The Calico Tiger

by Christian B. Garrison

Single copies of plays are sold for reading purposes only. The copying or duplicating of a play, or any part of play, by hand or by any other process, is an infringement of the copyright. Such infringement will be vigorously prosecuted.

Baker's Plays
c/o Samuel French, Inc.
45 West 25 Street
New York, NY 10010
bakersplays.com

NOTICE

This book is offered for sale at the price quoted only on the understanding that, if any additional copies of the whole or any part are necessary for its production, such additional copies will be purchased. The attention of all purchasers is directed to the following: this work is fully protected under the copyright laws of the United States of America, the British Commonwealth, including Canada, and all other countries of the Copyright Union. Violations of the Copyright Law are punishable by fine or imprisonment, or both. The copying or duplication of this work or any part of this work, by hand or by any process, is an infringement of the copyright and will be vigorously prosecuted.

This play may not be produced by amateurs or professionals for public or private performance without first submitting application for performing rights. Licensing fees are due on all performances whether for charity or gain, or whether admission is charged or not. Since performance of this play without the payment of the licensing fee renders anybody participating liable to severe penalties imposed by the law, anybody acting in this play should be sure, before doing so, that the licensing fee has been paid. Professional rights, reading rights, radio broadcasting, television and all mechanical rights, etc. are strictly reserved. Application for performing rights should be made directly to BAKER'S PLAYS.

No one shall commit or authorize any act or omission by which the copyright of, or the right to copyright, this play may be impaired. No one shall make any changes in this play for the purpose of production.

Publication of this play does not imply availability for performance. Both amateurs and professionals considering a production are strongly advised in their own interest to apply to Baker's Plays for written permission before starting rehearsals, advertising, or booking a theatre.

Whenever the play is produced, the author's name must be carried in all publicity, advertising and programs. Also, the following notice must appear on all printed programs, "Produced by special arrangement with Baker's Plays."

Licensing fees for THE CALICO TIGER are based on a per performance rate and payable one week in advance of the production.

Please consult the Baker's Plays website at www.bakersplays.com or our current print catalogue for up to date licensing fee information.

Copyright © 1973 by Christian B. Garrison
Made in U.S.A.
All rights reserved.

THE CALICO TIGER
ISBN **978-0-87440-981-9**
#1024-B

THE CALICO TIGER

A One-Act Children's Play

For a Flexible Cast of Eight
and Extras as Desired

CHARACTERS

THE WISEONE

JEROME TIGER

BIG MONKEY

LITTLE MONKEY NO. 1

LITTLE MONKEY NO. 2

ELEPHANT

RHINOCEROS

KING COBRA

BIRD OF PARADISE

A HUNTER

TIME: The present.

PLACE: Somewhere in the jungle.

PRODUCTION NOTES

The basic staging requires only several stepladders, a number of large paper cut-out leaves, sufficient light to illuminate the actors and simple costumes. These may be pajamas dyed and decorated to resemble animal skins, and paper bag or papier-mache half-masks, which cover the eyes and the top of the head with an animal face and ears, but which leave the lower part of the actor's face exposed.

The cut-out leaves should be easily attached to the step-ladders; early in the play the cast 'assembles' the forest before the audience. If the cast is small, this operation can be done energetically by the principal characters. If a sort of 'chorus' is desired, additional actors may be used to constitute the forest. In this case, they should also be costumed as animals. When they assemble the forest, they hold the leaves and branches in their hands rather than fastening them permanently to the ladders, and these actors remain on the ladders for the duration of the show. From here they can wave the branches to suit the action, simulating rain, wind, sunshine, covering over principal actors who wish to 'hide,' and so forth. They may even provide additional shouting in crowd scenes, sound effects for the weather. In any case, they should watch the action of the play intently, as its outcome affects their lives in the forest as well.

Additional variations, more elaborate costuming [always leaving the actors free for athletic movement], light and sound effects may be added at the director's discretion. If desired, ELEPHANT may even be a two-man costume, chinese-dragon style.

THE CALICO TIGER

SCENE: The stage is bathed in subdued twilight. We hear a melodic, Indian raga played on a sitar. It is slow, enchanting and lyrical.

AT RISE OF CURTAIN: Enter WISEONE. He is old and bent with age. His hair is long and snow-white, as is his beard. He supports himself in his slow, gingerly walk with a long staff. He wears a long, white Indian robe, and is truly the epitome of a wiseman. He crosses downstage and studies various members in the audience intently. OPTIONAL: He waves his staff and there is a sudden flash and puff of smoke from a flashpot secreted onstage. He addresses the audience.

WISEONE. Do you know who I am? Do you? [Wait for audience reaction. If desired, he may play with some simple magic effect, such as a color-changing handkerchief, as he speaks.] I am the **Wiseone!** Some call me a wizard, a magician, and a conjurer. I travel about the countryside dispensing wisdom and advice. I can do magic when I **want** to, but what I like most of all is telling stories. Do you want to hear a story? Good. For I am about to tell you one. [Raising his arms majestically] Many years ago, deep in the jungle . . Oops, that reminds me! We need a **jungle**. [Waving his staff] Let there be a jungle!

[Enter the jungle in the form of many children, each carrying some type of foliage, all yammering and screeching like jungle animals. Some scramble upstage to climb the ladders. They hold up their tree limbs and other foliage and are the trees for our jungle. Several others, with huge, plastic elephant-ear leaves, cross right center, left center and down left to position themselves. Then, all become still and quiet.]

No tropical jungle is complete without a bright, bright sun to make everything hot and steamy.

[A child enters carrying a large sun cutout from up-left and crosses to exit up right, as the lights dim up to a very bright full. The animals stretch and yawn in the sun.]

That's magic . . . Where were we? I keep forgetting! Oh, yes, our story! Many years ago, deep in the jungle, there lived a **Tiger.**

[Enter JEROME TIGER. He bows profusely to the audience and struts around the stage as the WISEONE narrates.]

His name was Jerome.
JEROME. That's me!
WISEONE. At least, that's what **he** called himself. Nobody else called him anything except **Tiger.** They did not ever get close enough to him to learn his name, because all the other animals were **afraid** of him. Jerome Tiger would stand in the middle of the jungle and **roar.** [Lights dim down on the WISEONE as JEROME lets out a tremendous roar.]
JEROME. [Roaring] Jerome's the name, scaring people's my game! Watch **this!**

[He runs downstage and roars at the audience, beating his chest, then giggles and hides by the proscenium

arch. The other characters enter from all directions at a
run. Two LITTLE MONKEYS scamper on followed by
BIG MONKEY. KING COBRA slithers on in a hurry.
RHINOCEROS scoots onstage followed by ELEPHANT
who squeals in a high pitch. BIRD OF PARADISE enters
slapping and squawking. They all run about making their
own particular cries and bump into each other in the
pandemonium of trying to find places to hide. RHINO
and ELEPHANT keep bumping into each other.]

RHINO. Get out of my way, fatty!
ELEPHANT. [Squealing] I'm scared! Tiger is coming to eat
    me up for sure! [The others have taken refuge. RHINO
    hides behind a tree, leaving only a small clump of elephant
    ears for ELEPHANT to hide behind, but ELEPHANT wants
    the tree to hide behind.]
RHINO. I've got this hiding place! Go find your own!
ELEPHANT. But I'm bigger than you, and I need a big hiding
    place!
RHINO. Go away! Hide over there. [Reluctantly ELEPHANT
    darts to the clump of elephant ears, not very well hidden at
    all. She hops up and down in fear. JEROME roars again,
    ELEPHANT shrieks and crouches, completely undone.]
ELEPHANT. Tiger will catch me for sure!

    [JEROME enters with a roar.]

JEROME. I'm the **fiercest** one around! [To audience, point-
    ing a thumb over his shoulder] They're all hiding from me.
    I am rather **mean** and **fierce** and **frightening.** Right? [Roar]
    Right? Now, where could they all be hiding? Let's see: Big
    Monkey and all of the little monkeys are hiding high in the
    trees. Rhinoceros went crashing through the tall grass to get
    away. King Cobra must have curled up into a ball to hide,
    and Bird of Paradise is somewhere with her feathers all ruf-
    fled and trembling. All of them scared, heh, heh! [Some-

thing occurs to him; he speaks more confidentially] Being
mean and fierce is fun for me, but I just realized: I don't
have any **friends!** Why doesn't anyone like me? I mean, I
never **gobble up** any of the others like most tigers would do.
[Shadow-boxing] I just punch 'em around a bit . . . [His
fake punches provoke new squeals of fear from ELEPHANT.
JEROME crouches suddenly and listens.] What's that I hear?
Sounds like Elephant whining away. [Crossing to clump of
foliage.] The sounds are coming from over there! [He darts
to the foliage where ELEPHANT is hiding. Frantic, ELE-
PHANT tries to make herself very small. JEROME stands
and strolls **very** casually around the foliage, whistling. ELE-
PHANT hugs the floor, circling the foliage on the opposite
side to stay hidden.   JEROME speaks for ELEPHANT's
benefit **very** casually.] Oh, if I catch that ponderous pach-
yderm, I'm going to tear her to bits with my razor sharp
claws. I'll bite her trunk with my needle sharp teeth. [Sud-
denly charging straight at her] I'll tear her limb from limb!
[At that, ELEPHANT lets out a frightened shriek and squeal.
JEROME chases and teases her.] Booga-booga-booga! [He
chases her about the stage as the others ad. lib. words of en-
couragement to the fleeing ELEPHANT.

     She finally exits squealing with JEROME roaring
right behind. BIG MONKEY comes down out of his
tree. He signals all-clear to the others, who come out
cautiously.]

BIRD OF PARADISE. What are we going to do?
LITTLE MONKEY NO. 1. I'm scared!
KING COBRA. **You're** scared?! What about me? At least you
can hide in the trees. I can't even get a good night's rest for
fear Tiger will be out walking and **step** on me while I'm
asleep.
BIG MONKEY. [Pacing back and forth] We've got to have a
plan.

BIRD OF PARADISE. Well, **my** plan is to move to another jungle. I'm so nervous now my feathers are falling out!

RHINO. At least you can **fly**. I have to stay on the ground all the time, and you know I don't **see** too well. I might walk right into Tiger one day, and he would like nothing better than to beat me up and even knock my beautiful **horn** off my nose!

LITTLE MONKEY NO. 2. I'm with Bird of Paradise. I say we move to another jungle.

BIG MONKEY. [Pacing and thinking] We need a plan.

OTHERS. [In unison] You've said that already!

BIG MONKEY. **Quiet!** I need to think.

RHINO. I'm too **scared** to be quiet.

LITTLE MONKEYS. We need something so we won't be afraid to come down out of the trees.

BIRD OF PARADISE. And so I won't get nervous and my feathers all fall out.

KING COBRA. And so I won't be stepped on in my sleep.

RHINO. And so I won't have to worry about bumping into Tiger. [They all burst into loud chatter, ad libbing their fears and concern.]

BIG MONKEY. Quiet! QUIET! Now just calm down and let's **think** of something. [All the animals take thinking postures for a moment, obviously working very hard.]

LITTLE MONKEY NO. 1. I wish I were a **wizard** and knew magic. I could turn Tiger into a banana. [He thinks again.]

LITTLE MONKEY NO. 2. Then I could **peel** him and **chew him up.** [Thinks again.]

RHINO. Or turn him into a **bush**, and I could **run over** him. [Thinks again.]

BIRD OF PARADISE. Or turn him into a **worm**, and I could **peck** him. [Thinks again.]

KING COBRA. Or turn him into a **mouse**, and I could **eat** him. [Thinks again.]

LITTLE MONKEY NO. 2. [Jumping up and down] Oh, if, if, if . . .

LITTLE MONKEY NO. 1. [Jumping up and down too] Yes,
  if, if, if I were a magician.

         [ELEPHANT enters. She is covered with large band-
         aids. Her trunk is in a sling and she is simpering and
         moaning.]

BIRD OF PARADISE. [Rushing to greet her] Oh, poor, poor
  Elephant. Did he hurt you?
KING COBRA. Why else would she be wearing all those band-
  ages?
ELEPHANT. [Moaning] Oh, he hurt me . . .
LITTLE MONKEY NO. 1. What did he do?
ELEPHANT. He did just what he said he would. First, he
  clawed me with those razor sharp claws of his [She makes
  a clawing gesture and sound] . . .
OTHERS. Yes? Then what?
ELEPHANT. Then he threw me on the ground . . . [She illu-
  strates violently.]
OTHERS. And then?
ELEPHANT. And then he **bit** my trunk with his needle sharp
  teeth! [She chomps on her own trunk, then squeals and
  weeps. The others react with shudders and ooohs and aahhs.]
BIG MONKEY. You're a big, fat scaredy-cat, Elephant! [With
  that, ELEPHANT breaks into great gales of tears and loud
  sobbings.]
RHINO. Now you've done it, Big Monkey. You know how
  hard it is to get Elephant to stop crying once she's started.
BIG MONKEY. You're a big, fat scaredy-cat, too! [Now
  RHINO starts roaring. BIG MONKEY plugs his ears with
  his fingers.] Quiet! Both of you, **shut up!** [Their cries
  subside to a sniffling.] I think I've got a plan. [To LITTLE
  MONKEY NO. 1] What was it you said about magic?
LITTLE MONKEY NO. 1. Uh . . . I don't remember.
LITTLE MONKEY NO. 2. You said you wish you were a wiz-
  ard so you could make magic. [He bops MONKEY NO. 1

on the head.]
LITTLE MONKEY NO. 1. Oh! [The bop brought the idea
    back.] That's right. So I could turn Tiger into a banana!
RHINO. Or a bush!
BIRD OF PARADISE. Or a worm!
KING COBRA. Or a mouse!
BIG MONKEY. That's it! That's what we'll do. We'll make
    magic.
OTHERS. Yes! We'll make magic! [They dance about in
    glee, and in unison they freeze when they realize:]
ELEPHANT. **How?**
BIRD OF PARADISE. Big Monkey, how are we going to
    make magic? **We're** not wizards.
RHINO. We don't know any magic.
KING COBRA. That's right. All I know is how to stick out
    my tongue and eat mice. [He illustrates, gobbling.]
ELEPHANT. All I can do is eat peanuts, and I can't even do
    that now that my trunk is broken.
LITTLE MONKEYS. We don't know any magic.
BIG MONKEY. [Proudly] I know a wizard. [All spin around]
RHINO. You do?
ALL. Who?
BIG MONKEY. And he knows how to perform all kinds of
    magic!
BIRD OF PARADISE. Who is he?
BIG MONKEY. [Dramatically] People call him **the Wiseone.**
KING COBRA. Let's go fetch him.
BIG MONKEY. [Darkly] I don't know where he is. [ELE-
    PHANT grabs BIG MONKEY and breaks into tears again.]
    Stop crying on me! You're getting my fur wet!

    [Suddenly, from offstage, JEROME TIGER gives a
    great roar, and all of the animals freeze. JEROME enters
    roaring. They all begin running about to get away. JER-
    OME gives chase, the chase being a stylized, slapstick
    ballet of sorts. The music comes up. JEROME almost

catches first one and then another of the animals. The number ends with all of the animals taking flight off-stage when Jerome trips and falls sprawling. He gets up slowly, dusts himself off and addresses audience.]

JEROME. Did you see them run? I told you I was the fiercest one around. [Strutting] I can frighten **anyone**. Man or beast. In fact, news of my fierceness has probably traveled the world over. I'll bet I can even frighten YOU!

[He roars at the audience and then laughs and is about to roar again when he notices the WISEONE entering upstage.]

What's this? **A person**. I'll frighten him out of his wits, heh, heh. Shhh! I'll hide behind this bush and jump out on him when he passes by. [He secrets himself behind a bush as the WISEONE crosses downstage, closer and closer. To audience:] Shhh! [The WISEONE reaches JEROME's position, and just as JEROME is about to pounce, the WISEONE turns around. JEROME quickly and quietly jumps behind the WISEONE, without being detected. As the WISEONE turns about to look, JEROME stays behind him.]

WISEONE. I thought I heard something. One must be care-ful when traveling through the jungle. [Listening, hearing nothing.] Must have been the wind in the trees. [He walks a few more steps, with JEROME right behind him.] I **know** I heard something creeping up on me. Did **you**? [When he turns around JEROME jumps up and roars. The WISEONE doesn't budge. JEROME roars again, this time right in the old man's face. The WISEONE holds his ground.]

JEROME. I am Jerome Tiger! The fiercest one around!

WISEONE. [Calmly] I am the Wiseone, the **smartest** one around. [JEROME roars again, jumping straight up in the air and beating his chest. No response.]

JEROME. [Confused] You're supposed to quiver and quake
    when you see me.
WISEONE. Why should I quiver and quake?
JEROME. Because you're frightened. Scared.
WISEONE. [Chuckling] Me? Frightened of you?
JEROME. [Aside] This old man must be crazy. He's not at
    all scared. But **this** roar will get his knees knocking for sure.
    [JEROME fills his lungs with a deep breath, positions him-
    self one inch from the WISEONE's face, and is about to let
    out a big roar, when the WISEONE calmly taps JEROME on
    the head with his staff. This sends JEROME sprawling to
    the floor. He rubs his head.] Hey! That's not fair!
WISEONE. Why not?
JEROME. [Getting up] You hit me! You're supposed to be
    frightened when I growl and roar and show my teeth. Why
    aren't your knees knocking and your hands trembling?
WISEONE. [Yawning] Because I am **not** frightened when you
    growl and roar and show your teeth. That is why my knees
    are not knocking and my hands trembling. [Aside, but for
    JEROME's benefit.] In fact, he is nothing more than an
    overgrown pussy cat!
JEROME. [Frustrated and pushy] I'll roar louder!
WISEONE. And I'll pulverize you to powder.
JEROME. I'll tear you up with my claws!
WISEONE. [Mocking] Then you will bite me with those
    powerful jaws?
JEROME. [Flattered] That's right. You must have heard of
    me, wise old man. My jaws **are** powerful!
WISEONE. [Leading him on] I hear you are also very strong.
JEROME. Sure I am. [Flexing biceps] Feel that muscle.
WISEONE. I hear you are very intelligent.
JEROME. [Enjoying the flattery] I guess I'm about the
    smartest animal in the jungle. I can add, subtract, multiply,
    and divide.
WISEONE. Amazing!
JEROME. I can even stand on my head and count to ten.

WISEONE. Now **that** is hard to believe.

JEROME. [Drawing back a fist] You don't believe me?

WISEONE. [Wisely] Oh, I believe you. I just **never** have seen so fierce a tiger as you.

JEROME. [Putting up his dukes and shadow boxing] I'd rather beat you up, old one.

WISEONE. Why not show me how intelligent you are, **then** beat me up?

JEROME. Okay! Give me a problem.

WISEONE. What is three and one-half plus one-half?

JEROME. Hah! That's easy. [Thinking] Hmmmm. Three and one-half plus one-half. [Aside] Why didn't he ask me two plus two. I know that one. [To WISEONE] Give me four guesses.

WISEONE. Very well.

JEROME. One?

WISEONE. No.

JEROME. Two?

WISEONE. No.

JEROME. [Worried] Three?

WISEONE. No.

JEROME. Four!

WISEONE. Very good!

JEROME. I told you I was smart. [Putting up his dukes again] Now I'm going to beat you up.

WISEONE. [Doubtful] Can you really stand on your head and count to ten?

JEROME. Sure.

WISEONE. Astounding! Why not show me, and **then** beat me up?

JEROME. [Waving his dukes] I'd rather beat you up now.

WISEONE. Well, Jerome, if you were the clever tiger you say you are, you wouldn't mind standing on your head and counting to ten, to **prove** how clever you are.

JEROME. All right, I'll show you. [JEROME gets on the floor and tries to stand on his head, failing the first few tries.] It's been a while since I've done this. [Falling over again.] I'm a little out of practice. [He tries again and manages to get up shakily.] One . . . two . . . three . . . uh . . what comes after four? Don't tell me, I'll get it. Five! . . . Six . . .

[As JEROME is counting, the WISEONE tiptoes all the way offstage.]

Seven . . . uh . . . I don't remember that one. [He begins to totter and then falls over with a bump, then gets up.] Well, I told you I was a little out of prac . . . [Looks about] Where did he go? [Furious] He **tricked** me! Nobody tricks the great Jerome Tiger and gets away with it! Wait till I get my hands on that crazy old man!

[JEROME exits in high dudgeon. KING COBRA pokes his head out from the forest, flicking his tongue. He looks both ways.]

KING COBRA. Is the coast clear? Is he gone? [Another look] He's gone! [Slithering out excitedly.] Big Monkey! Where are you? He was here! The old wizard was here. Big Monkey! I saw the Wiseone!

[Other ANIMALS come out of hiding, including BIG MONKEY.]

I saw him, Big Monkey. He was **right here!**
BIG MONKEY. Who was? Who was?
KING COBRA. The old man! The Wiseone! [The others gather around to listen, astonished.]
BIG MONKEY. Why do you think this old man is the Wise-one?
KING COBRA. He wasn't afraid of Tiger at **all!** [The others gasp in amazement.]

ELEPHANT. He didn't shake and tremble, even a little teeny
   bit?
KING COBRA. The wise old man actually knocked Tiger
   down! That's right! He hit Tiger on the head with a long
   staff. [Laughing] You should have seen Tiger all sprawled
   out like a baby! [They all howl at the thought of it.] That's
   not all. He made Tiger **stand on his head and count to ten!**
   [They all gibber at the thought.]
BIG MONKEY. [Impressed] He **must** be the Wiseone, the
   true wizard the people in the village speak of!
ELEPHANT. Let's find him!
RHINO. [About to charge off] Yes! We must find him.
BIG MONKEY. Wait, Rhinoceros! You can't go charging off
   without knowing where you're going.
RHINO. [Thinking this over] You're right.
BIG MONKEY. [To KING COBRA] Which way did the Wise-
   one go?
KING COBRA. That way. [ALL of the animals stampede off
   excitedly en masse when BIG MONKEY stops them.]
BIG MONKEY. Whoa! Hold on there, friends.
ELEPHANT. [Stamping] We have to find the Wiseone!
BIG MONKEY. But you have to look in the right place! [Sud-
   denly there is a tremendous roar offstage. The result is
   immediate panic among the animals, who lurch about squeal-
   ing and hiding. They are all hidden when we hear another
   roar.

   The WISEONE enters. He stops, looks about and
   lets out a big tiger-sounding roar. He listens, then
   laughs loudly. BIG MONKEY peeks out from behind
   a bush, then another animal and another, until all are
   cautiously peering at the WISEONE.]

KING COBRA. That's him! It's the Wiseone!

   [They all crawl out from hiding, and BIG MONKEY

crosses nervously to the WISEONE.]

BIG MONKEY. Are you the wizard?
WISEONE. I'm just a wise old man. Some call me Wiseone.
    Some call me a wizard.
LITTLE MONKEY NO. 1. [Boldly] Can you perform magic?
WISEONE. When I want to, although I prefer the magic of
    the **imagination** to the magic of pulling rabbits out of hats.
BIG MONKEY. Are we glad we found you!
WISEONE. I found **you.**
ELEPHANT. [Still trembling] We thought you were **Tiger!**
WISEONE. Why did you think that?
BIG MONKEY. Because we heard the roaring and the growling.
WISEONE. I prefer the magic of the **imagination.**
BIG MONKEY. [Scratching his head] Indeed you are the wise
    one, but what are you saying?
WISEONE. Is it a kind of **magic,** that all of you thought I was
    the tiger?
BIG MONKEY. [Scratching his head] Well . . . I guess . . .
ELEPHANT. [Excited] But we thought you were a wizard
    who can make the rains come and go at will . . .
RHINO. [Excited] And the winds stop and stand still . . .
BIRD OF PARADISE. [Excited] And things without wings
    float in the air high as a roof . . .
KING COBRA. [Excited] And make people vanish in a poof!
WISEONE. Why would you want **that** kind of magic?
BIG MONKEY. Because we need help to fight **Tiger!**
WISEONE. What help can I be? I am just an old man.
BIG MONKEY. You're a wizard of an old man.
ELEPHANT. [Incredulous] Aw, he's no wizard. He's just a
    crazy old man.
WISEONE. [Raising his staff] Shall I turn you into a puff
    of smoke for the wind to blow away? [They all oooh and
    aahh, backing away. ELEPHANT starts crying uncontrol-
    ably.]
WISEONE. Silence! [ELEPHANT stops her crying as sudden-

ly as she started.]
LITTLE MONKEY NO. 1. [Amazed] He made Elephant stop
    crying. He **is** a wizard!
WISEONE. Fear not, big friend. I shan't turn you into a puff
    of smoke for the wind to blow away.
ELEPHANT. [Groveling] Thank you! Thank you!
BIG MONKEY. We **know** you can do amazing things. You
    made Tiger stand on his head and count to ten. King Cobra
    saw you.
WISEONE. I know.
KING COBRA. You know?
WISEONE. The jungle has a million eyes, always there, always
    watching. Besides, I heard you stick your tongue out to
    lick the air.
KING COBRA. [Flicking his tongue] Goodness me! I **did** do
    that.
BIG MONKEY. Oh, great Wiseone, please help us in our plight.
    Only **you** can help us.
WISEONE. No, no. The only magic I can do is give you advice.
    You yourselves must do whatever needs to be done.
BIG MONKEY. What do you advise we do?
WISEONE. Did you think I was Tiger?
BIG MONKEY. Why, yes, but . . .
WISEONE. Did you shrink in fear and run for cover when you
    heard me growling?
BIRD OF PARADISE. Yes, but . . .
WISEONE. [Walking away] Well, then. You have solved your
    own problem.
BIG MONKEY. [Confused] I don't understand. [To audience]
    Do you? [Running to WISEONE] Tell us the wisdom in
    your words, great wise one.
WISEONE. [Holding out his arms and chanting]
        Things are not always as they seem.
        Does a tiger always bite or a diamond always gleam?
        Tiger's roar is not the fiercest one around,
        Since a **bigger** tiger makes a **fiercer** sound.

[The WISEONE walks away as they stand there in confused silence, then all scramble after him.]

ALL. Wait!

WISEONE. [Turning] I have told you all you need to know. Work the magic of the imagination; conjure up the solution from inside your own hearts and heads. [He tries to walk away again.]

BIG MONKEY. [Pursuing] We don't understand what to do!

WISEONE. Stop! I can give you advice; you must work your own magic by using your own wisdom.

[He exits. OPTIONAL: He waves his staff and he is gone in a flash and a puff of smoke. They all gawk and mumble among themselves.]

BIRD OF PARADISE. What did he mean, talking about diamonds and such?

RHINO. I hate riddles!

BIG MONKEY. Think, everybody! [Some pace and numble, others 'think' as before.]

RHINO. [To audience] I hate riddles. Can you figure it out? [He works with the audience for a response.]

BIG MONKEY. [Suddenly] I have it!

KING COBRA. What is it!?

BIG MONKEY. Listen carefully: 'Things are not always as they seem. Does a tiger always bite or a diamond always gleam?'

RHINO. That's no answer. That's the riddle!

BIG MONKEY. Hush! [To audience] Listen and think: 'Tiger's roar is not the fiercest one around. Since a **bigger** tiger makes a **fiercer** sound.' Don't you see?

ELEPHANT. No.

BIG MONKEY. What if **we** all made a roar at the same time? Why, such a roar would strike fear in even the meanest tiger!

LITTLE MONKEY NO. 2. That's it, Big Monkey!

LITTLE MONKEY NO. 1. We'll **roar**.

BIRD OF PARADISE. And **roar.**
ALL. And ROAR!   [Suddenly, from offstage comes JEROME's
    roaring.]
ELEPHANT. Eeek! What do we do?
BIG MONKEY. Hide over there, and when he comes by, we
    let out a roar that will make his fur stand on end!

[They all hide as JEROME strolls onstage.]

JEROME. Ho, hum. I'm bored. What I need is to find some-
    one to frighten. [All at once, all of the hidden animals let
    out a great roaring. JEROME does a somersault, the sound
    of the roar is so great.] Great goodness me! I've never
    heard such a fierce-sounding roar in my life! The tiger who
    belongs to **that** roar must be as big as a house! I'd better
    not hang around to see, for whatever it is might get me!

[He exits in a hurry. The animals rush out and cross
    to wings, roaring after him, waving fists and jeering. In
    the meantime, JEROME enters from the opposite side of
    the stage. He is angry at having been duped and takes
    great delight in sneaking up on them from behind. He
    stops, takes a stance, arms akimbo and one foot tapping.
    They stop roaring and begin laughing. They turn around
    to see JEROME right there. They scream and flee off-
    stage with JEROME in pursuit. BIG MONKEY rushes
    downstage to address the audience.]

BIG MONKEY. That was a close one! I must find the Wise-
    one! Will we ever be able to live in peace with Tiger?

[He runs down left calling 'Wiseone! Wiseone!' Upon
    his exit, JEROME enters upright. He is huffing and puff-
    ing.]

JEROME. Missed them! I wish those sneaky little monkeys

couldn't climb trees. [Yawning] Oh, me, all that chasing has made me sleepy. What I need is an old-fashioned nap. Do you know what tigers like even better than growling and scaring folks? Sleep! We love to sleep, so I think I'll lie down over here behind this tree and take a long, peaceful nap.

[He crosses upstage and disappears behind a tree, settling with a whole-body yawn. At that moment, the WISEONE enters and crosses downstage to sit on the stage apron. He begins rubbing his feet.]

WISEONE. An old man's feet get tired when he spends his time walking through the jungle being wise and answering all kinds of questions from all kinds of creatures. I wonder how the other animals are getting along with Jerome Tiger? If they just would bother to find out about one another, they would become fast friends. [Rising] Have you ever known someone you thought you did not like at all? And then you found out more about that person and realized you liked him after all? [Chuckling] That goes to show you how silly we all are sometimes. We are always judging things by what is on the **outside.**

[BIG MONKEY enters swinging on a vine, just missing the WISEONE.]

BIG MONKEY. Wiseone! I was on my way to find you.
WISEONE. You almost knocked me down!
BIG MONKEY. I had to find you! Our plan to trick Tiger failed.
WISEONE. Oh?
BIG MONKEY. Can't you just go 'Abra-Kadabra. Poof!' and make Tiger disappear?
WISEONE. I can.
BIG MONKEY. You will?

WISEONE. I won't.

BIG MONKEY. Why?

WISEONE. Because I **like** Jerome Tiger, and you would too if you knew him better.

BIG MONKEY. [Making a face] **Jerome** Tiger?

WISEONE. See? You think better of him already now that you know his name.

BIG MONKEY. But I'm still frightened of him.

WISEONE. [Putting a hand on his shoulder] **Courage** is not something that is on the outside. Courage comes from inside here. From the heart. That is the only **magic** you need to know. Goodbye, Big Monkey. I must be going.

[The WISEONE exits.]

BIG MONKEY. Wait ... [Suddenly there is loud snorings coming from behind the tree. BIG MONKEY jumps when he hears it.] What's that? Sounds like that rascal Tiger! [He carefully sneaks upstage to peer behind the tree.] It **is** Tiger! He's asleep. [Giggling] His snoring is as loud as his roaring! [Running downstage to the audience] Now that he's asleep, I have my chance! But what to do? Hmmmm. [He 'thinks.'] The magic of the imagination. I'll creep up on him and tie his feet with a rope! No. I'll dig a hole and put him in it! No. I'll shave off his fur so he'll catch cold! [Shivering] Ooo! I'm afraid to touch him! **I've got it!** [Leaping straight up in the air, somersaults and quickly runs behind a tree and returns in a split-second with a paint can -- which is actually empty -- and brush. He disappears behind the tree where JEROME is sleeping. We hear JEROME's loud snoring. The LITTLE MONKEYS scamper onstage and watch the hidden action, jumping, pointing and giggling. Then BIG MONKEY emerges, and says to the little monkeys:] Shhh! The Wiseone was right. The imagination **is** the best magic. No one will fear Tiger now.

[JEROME makes sounds of waking up. BIG MONK-
EY takes a hasty last look, then ushers the others off
and exits. Amidst yawnings and sputterings JEROME
appears. His nice orange and black stripes are no longer
there. Instead, he is **calico** from head to toe -- he has
changed costumes behind the bush.]

JEROME. Ho, hum. What a nice nap! After such a restful
nap, I like to find someone and frighten the wits out of
him. Let's see . . .

[ELEPHANT enters, casually walking along throwing
peanuts in the air and trying to catch them in her mouth.
JEROME spys her, lurches over to her and starts to let
out a roar when ELEPHANT sees him and breaks into
huge laughter. JEROME is confused.]

Why are you laughing? [ELEPHANT cannot answer because
of her uncontrollable laughter. She hoots and howls, pointing at JEROME. He roars:] You are supposed to quake
and shake when you see me! [ELEPHANT falls on her back
and kicks her feet in the air with laughter.] Am I dreaming?
This fat elephant is supposed to be howling with fear, not
laughter!

[The other animals enter from different parts of the
stage to see the Calico Tiger, and they begin laughing
and ad libbing their surprise and mirth.]

What is this? [Frustrated] **I am Jerome Tiger!** I'm the
fiercest one around!
BIG MONKEY. [Extending hand to shake] **Hi, Jerome,** glad
to know you. I'm Big Monkey. And this is Little Monkey
Number 1.
LITTLE MONKEY No. 1. Hi.
BIG MONKEY. And this is Little Monkey Number 2.

LITTLE MONKEY NO. 2. [Giggling] Nice to meet you.

BIG MONKEY. And over here is Rhinoceros.

RHINO. Welcome to our jungle.

BIG MONKEY. And Bird of Paradise.

BIRD OF PARADISE. [Fluttering past] Hiya, Jerome.

BIG MONKEY. And down here is King Cobra.

KING COBRA. Greetings!

ELEPHANT. [Recovering] Have a peanut!

JEROME. Why aren't you afraid of me?

BIG MONKEY. Who could be afraid of **you?**

JEROME. But, I'm Jerome Tiger, and I'm fierce, and mean
    and strong!

RHINO. But we want to be your friend.

JEROME. I don't **want** any friends!

ELEPHANT. Everybody needs friends. Have a peanut.

JEROME. [Growing more horrified] I don't want a peanut!

LITTLE MONKEY NO. 2. [Holding his arm and jumping up
    and down.] Be our friend, Jerome.

LITTLE MONKEY NO. 1. [On his other arm] Jerome's a
    nice name.

BIRD OF PARADISE. And you're a beautiful **Calico,** too!

JEROME. Calico? [He looks at himself] A-a-a-agh! What
    happened to my stripes? [Holding his belly] I'm sick! I
    have a tropical disease! My stripes fell off! What do I do?
    What do I do?

ALL. **Be our friend!**

JEROME. But I . . . Your friend? But I'm supposed to be
    mean and . . . [Carefully and bewilderingly inspecting his
    new calico fur] Calico! Have you ever seen anything so
    silly? I'm miserable. If only I had my old stripes back,
    then I'd know who I was. This calico is rather enchanting . .
    . . [Bursting into tears] But I want my stripes back! [He
    turns and walks away, bawling.]

BIG MONKEY. [Pursuing] Wait a minute! Jerome!

JEROME. [Fleeing, still bawling] Get away from me!

BIG MONKEY. No, wait a minute! I just want to . . .

[They are gone. The OTHERS cluster for a confer-
ence, except for the LITTLE MONKEYS, who bring
out a coconut from behind a tree -- it is a soft, brown
rubber ball -- and play catch with it.]

BIRD OF PARADISE. Where is Big Monkey going?
RHINO. I don't know! Do you think it's serious?
ELEPHANT. Maybe he's worried about the rainy season com-
ing up.
RHINO. You're dumb. [ELEPHANT whimpers.]
LITTLE MONKEY NO. 1. Throw me the coconut. [LITTLE
MONKEY NO. 2 throws the coconut, but it is too high, and
it sails offstage. LITTLE MONKEY NO. 1 watches the
sailing coconut.] Uh-oh.
LITTLE MONKEY NO. 2. **Oh no!**

[Both MONKEYS watch in horror, then curl up and
cover their heads in horror. A terrible crash offstage.
BIG MONKEY crawls on, dizzy, holding the coconut.]

BIG MONKEY. You guys ought to look where you're throwing
things. You hit me right on the head!
LITTLE MONKEYS. [Scampering away with fear] Sorry!
Sorry!
RHINO. Where have you been?
BIG MONKEY. Thinking.
ELEPHANT. Boy, **everybody's** doing that!
BIRD OF PARADISE. About what?
BIG MONKEY. About our calico tiger.
KING COBRA. Ever since the Wiseone used his magic and
turned Tiger into calico, Tiger's been hiding.
LITTLE MONKEY NO. 2. Yeah. We wanted him to play with
us.
BIG MONKEY. Now all of you listen. You have been wonder-
ing why I'm worried, right?
ELEPHANT. Well, you **are** acting a little strange.

BIG MONKEY. I'm worried about the rainy season.
ELEPHANT. Told you so!
RHINO. But the rainy season comes every year.
BIG MONKEY. This time will be **different**.
BIRD OF PARADISE. If you're worried about getting wet,
    you may stay in my nice, dry nest.
BIG MONKEY. **I'm** not worried about getting wet.
KING COBRA. Why **are** you worried then?
ELEPHANT. Tell us. I'm all ears.
BIG MONKEY. How many of you are afraid of Jerome?
ELEPHANT. [After a pause] Uh, who's Jerome?
BIG MONKEY. Don't tell me you've forgotten his name
    already?!
KING COBRA. Jerome who?
BIG MONKEY. Jerome **Tiger,** you bird-brain!
BIRD OF PARADISE. I beg your pardon!
BIG MONKEY. Sorry, Bird of Paradise. How can you forget
    a friend's name?
ELEPHANT. He's no friend of mine. He used to tweak my
    trunk.
BIG MONKEY. Does he any more?
ELEPHANT. Well, no . . .
KING COBRA. He used to step on me when I napped.
BIG MONKEY. Does he any more?
KING COBRA. Well, no . . .
BIG MONKEY. If you're not afraid of him, why don't you
    want to be his friend?
LITTLE MONKEY NO. 2. Because he **used** to scare us and
    beat us up.
BIG MONKEY. And **you** hit me on the head with a coconut,
    but I don't hold that against you.
LITTLE MONKEY NO. 1. [Jumping up and down] I'm not
    afraid of Jerome Tiger now that he's a calico tiger.
KING COBRA. Hush. Thank goodness the Wiseone used his
    magic to turn Jerome into a calico tiger.
BIG MONKEY. The Wiseone didn't use his magic on Jerome.

I did.
ALL. [Drawing back] Huh?
BIG MONKEY. I **painted** him calico.
ALL. You **what?**
BIG MONKEY. I painted him.
RHINO. That means when it rains . . .
BIG MONKEY. When it rains, the paint will **wash off**, and
    Jerome will realize it **wasn't** the Wiseone's magic at all.
ALL. [Looking at the sky] Uh-oh.
BIG MONKEY. Now you know why I'm worried. And you
    know how tigers love water. Jerome will be out playing in
    the rain, and for sure the paint will wash off!
LITTLE MONKEY NO. 2. [Looking offstage] Aaak! Here he
    comes now!

[They all run about in confusion as JEROME enters.
He looks at them, then he looks at himself to see if he
has his stripes back. He is still calico and is confused.]

BIG MONKEY. [Nervous] Oh, hi there, Jerome. Uh, fancy
    meeting you here.
JEROME. [Happily] Well, I've decided I like being a **calico**
    tiger. Now I have a lot of friends. Let's play, everybody!
BIG MONKEY. You certainly are looking well, Jerome.
JEROME. [Indicating others, who are running about] What's
    wrong with them?
BIG MONKEY. [Nervous] Who?
JEROME. Them.
BIG MONKEY. Oh, them! Uh . . . Exercising. That's it. Ex-
    ercising.
JEROME. Hmmmm. If I didn't know better, I'd think they
    were frightened of **me** again.
BIG MONKEY. [Growing more nervous] Frightened of you?
    Heh, heh.
JEROME. I want to play too. I love exercise! [He falls in be-
    hind the others who are running about in a large circle try-

ing to get away. As he does, they go faster and faster in an attempt to stay ahead. He keeps up, and finally they all fall over exhausted and panting. JEROME crawls to BIG MON-KEY, exhausted.]

Oh, boy! That was fun. Are you sure you're not nervous about something?

BIG MONKEY. Nervous? Me? Oh, no. Uh . . . I'm just get-ting excited about the rain.

JEROME. Me too! I can't wait till the rainy season starts. I love to play in the rain and roll around in the cool pools of water.

BIG MONKEY. That's what I was afraid of.

JEROME. Huh?

BIG MONKEY. Nothing!

JEROME. Oh, how I love the rainy season. Should be here any day now. [He puts his arm around BIG MONKEY in a friendly gesture. BIG MONKEY makes a terrible face.] You know, I **like** being calico like this and having **friends** and all. I'm glad I don't have stripes anymore.

BIG MONKEY. [Gulping] Really?

JEROME. Yeah. Because I can't scare anybody anymore now that I'm a calico tiger. And because I don't scare anybody, I have friends. [There is a sudden clap of thunder and flash-es of lightning.] Rejoice! Here come the rains!

[The other ANIMALS flee for shelter among the trees.]

BIG MONKEY. And there go the animals!

[JEROME crosses to some foliage and takes out a bar of soap and a bath brush as the thunder and lightning continue. The children on the ladders representing the trees begin throwing handfuls of confetti which shower down like rain. JEROME scrubs his back happily. All

but BIG MONKEY and JEROME have exited. BIG
MONKEY, downstage, covers his head from the rain.]

What's going to happen when he washes away that paint
and finds his stripes are under there? I know one thing:
This is no time to **monkey around!**

[He runs off. JEROME follows, saying:]

JEROME. Say, Big Monkey, have you got a toothbrush?

[The WISEONE enters from the other side, carrying
an embrella over his head.]

WISEONE. [To audience] Well, the rainy season started all
right. The rain made little drum beats on the leaves. The
rain droplets plunged into droplets and made rushing rivers
to float leaf-boats on. And what else did the rain do? The
rain washed away the calico, and JEROME got his stripes
back.

[JEROME, in his striped costume, enters upstage,
yawns loudly and lies down.]

Do you think the other animals will ever make friends with
Jerome Tiger? Shhh. Let's watch and see.

[He exits down R as the two LITTLE MONKEYS
enter L.]

LITTLE MONKEY NO. 1. Shhh! There's Jerome Tiger. Better not let him catch us!
LITTLE MONKEY NO. 2. We haven't had a moment's peace
since he got his stripes back. He wasn't such a bad fellow
in calico. He's been so angry because he was tricked into
thinking he was really calico that he says he's going to

gobble us all up if he catches us.

LITTLE MONKEY NO. 1. It gives me the **shudders** to think of it.

LITTLE MONKEY NO. 2. [They sneak closer to JEROME] If we could think of a way to scare Jerome Tiger badly enough, we could all live in peace.

LITTLE MONKEY NO. 1. Let's use our imaginations and come up with an idea, a plan.

LITTLE MONKEY NO. 2. I've got it. [JEROME sputters as if about to wake up.]

LITTLE MONKEY NO. 1. Shh! He's waking up. Let's get out of here.

[They exit as JEROME wakes and sits up abruptly, looking about.]

JEROME. I thought I heard voices. [Yawning] Must have been a dream.

[The WISEONE enters without the umbrella and sees JEROME.]

WISEONE. Hello, Jerome! I haven't seen you since the rainy season.

JEROME. You mean when I was that silly calico?

WISEONE. Oh, yes. That was very nice.

JEROME. Nice?! It was ridiculous! It was **humiliating!** Oh, it makes me mad. In fact, I'm so mad, I'm going to eat all of the other animals if I catch them!

WISEONE. [Pointing his staff toward JEROME] You'll have to admit that you had more friends when you were a calico tiger than you do now.

JEROME. True. And now I'm going to gobble them all up like any self-respecting tiger would do!

WISEONE. You are cantankerous and mean because you **think** that's the way you should act. Haven't **you** ever been

frightened?
JEROME. Me? What could frighten me?
WISEONE. [Ominous] **Man the hunter.**
JEROME. [Frightened] You mean . . .?
WISEONE. With his **guns!**
JEROME. Oh no! But **you're** a man.
WISEONE. Yes, but I am a **wise** man. I don't kill tigers.
JEROME. [Terrified] What can I do if the hunter comes into
   the jungle?
WISEONE. That is why you need friends, Jerome Tiger. Good-
   bye.

   [WISEONE exits. JEROME comes downstage,
   worried, and confides to audience:]

JEROME. It would be nice to have friends, especially at a time
   like that. But the others are all frightened of me in my
   stripes.

   [Suddenly, BIG MONKEY, ELEPHANT, KING
   COBRA, RHINO and BIRD OF PARADISE stampede
   onstage.]

ELEPHANT. **Run for your lives!**
RHINO. **Hunter!**
JEROME. What?
BIRD OF PARADISE. **Man with a gun!**
JEROME. [Spinning in terror] **Where?**
BIG MONKEY. **Run for your lives!**

   [They all exit leaving JEROME spinning onstage,
   confused. He runs about and then hides behind a bush
   as the two LITTLE MONKEYS enter, one on top of the
   other's shoulders, disguised as a hunter. They have on a
   long coat, a pith helmet and the top monkey carries a
   rifle. The disguise is quite good except for the bottom

monkey's tail sticking out from under the coat.]

JEROME. [Hiding behind one tree, then another] It **is** the
    hunter!
TOP MONKEY. [In a deep voice] Where is that tiger? I'll
    shoot him for sure, if I find him.
JEROME. Ooh! He's coming this way! [The **MONKEY-
    HUNTER** walks about as if looking for him. They play a
    serious hide-and-seek among the trees and foliage. JEROME
    ends up behind a clump of foliage and the **MONKEY-HUNT-
    ER** steps near, turning about to look. The tail is bobbing up
    and down from under the coat. JEROME runs downstage
    to audience] A tail? I've never seen a **man** with a tail! [He
    runs back and hides.]
TOP MONKEY. [In deep voice] Where **is** he? Where's that
    wretched tiger?
JEROME. [Running to audience again] People don't have
    tails like that. [Realizing] But **monkeys** do!
TOP MONKEY. I wonder where he could be.
JEROME. [Standing up menacingly] Why don't you try look-
    ing **behind** you? [The **MONKEY-HUNTER** turns around
    face to face with JEROME who roars, causing them to top-
    ple over. JEROME grabs the two of them.] So, you two
    pipsqueaks are trying to get tough, huh?
LITTLE MONKEY NO. 2. Uh-oh.
LITTLE MONKEY NO. 1. **Help!** [He faints into his brother's
    arms.]
JEROME. I'm going to have you two for my **supper!**
LITTLE MONKEY NO. 1. [Shaking] Are you sure you're
    hungry?
JEROME. Come to think of it, I've already eaten today.
LITTLE MONKEY NO. 2. [Waking right up] Since you're
    not hungry, you can let us go!
JEROME. Ha! I'll tie you to this tree and keep you until I
    am hungry. [He ties them to the tree with some vines.
    They yammer and gibber the entire time.   He holds up one

of their tails deliciously.] I'm sure I'll be hungry in a little
while.

[He exits, smacking his lips.]

LITTLE MONKEY NO. 1. Well, here's a fine mess you've
gotten us into. I told you it wouldn't work.
LITTLE MONKEY NO. 2. What'll we do now?   [The lights
dim a little.]
LITTLE MONKEY NO.1. The sun's going down!
LITTLE MONKEY NO. 2. [Weakly] Help! Hel-lp!

[BIG MONKEY enters.]

LITTLE MONKEY NO. 2. Big Monkey! Help!
LITTLE MONKEY NO. 1. Over here! Help us!
BIG MONKEY. [Standing in front of them with his arms
crossed.] How did this happen?
LITTLE MONKEY NO. 2. He did it!
LITTLE MONKEY NO. 1. **He** did it!
BIG MONKEY. Stop arguing and tell me what happened, or
I won't untie you.
LITTLE MONKEY NO. 1. We dressed up like a hunter to
frighten Tiger and he caught on.
LITTLE MONKEY NO. 2. He caught **us!**
BIG MONKEY. That wasn't a hunter? It was **you?**
LITTLE MONKEY NO. 2. [Proudly] That's right.
BIG MONKEY. I ought to leave you tied up forever!
LITTLE MONKEY NO. 1. No! Tiger will eat us for breakfast!
BIG MONKEY. You scared the rest of us half to death!
LITTLE MONKEY NO. 1. We only meant to scare Tiger.
BIG MONKEY. **Why, Elephant's still** crying.
LITTLE MONKEYS. [Together] We're sorry.
BIG MONKEY. [Untying them] All right. Let's go before
nightfall catches us here.

[They exit. JEROME re-enters, singing.]

JEROME. Tum-te-tum-tum . . .[Sings] Time for break-fast!
    Tum-te . . . [He sees they are gone.] . . What! What's going
    on here? They got away! Oooh, that makes me angry!

        [A real HUNTER enters. He wears a coat and a pith
    helmet and carries a rifle.]

HUNTER. [Looking about, says in a deep voice:] This looks
    like a good spot for tiger hunting. [Evil] I can't wait!
    [Spotting JEROME] Wait! Is that . . . Yes! That tiger's
    head will be perfect!
JEROME. [Spotting HUNTER] Those two silly monkeys are
    at it again! This time I'll teach them once and for all.
    [JEROME jumps behind the tree as the HUNTER closes in
    on him.]
HUNTER. I saw him; I know I did! The fiercest looking tiger
    I ever saw.
JEROME. I'll crack those two monkeys heads together. [JER-
    OME jumps out and grabs the HUNTER and they both
    tumble about on the floor.]
HUNTER. Ooof! He's got **me**!
JEROME. I've got you two!
HUNTER. You crazy beast, let go! [JEROME realizes the
    HUNTER is for real and he jumps back. The HUNTER
    grabs his rifle and holds it on JEROME.] Now, you wretch-
    ed beast, I've got you! [Taking aim] This will teach you
    to monkey around with me. [Just as the HUNTER is about
    to pull the trigger, a whole barrage of coconuts come from
    offstage to hit the HUNTER.] Ooof! What's this?

        [ALL of the animals enter, throwing and brandishing
    coconuts and making loud noises.   The HUNTER
    thrashes on the floor, calling:]

Help! The whole jungle's after me!
ALL. **Leave our jungle!**
HUNTER. [Crawling to get away] Help! Help!
ALL. [Throwing coconuts] **Go away!**

[The HUNTER finally escapes offstage. One of the
LITTLE MONKEYS puts up a 'Posted — No Hunting'
sign, and they all laugh and dance about. JEROME and
BIG MONKEY have exited.]

ELEPHANT. [Jumping up] Good riddance!
BIRD OF PARADISE. [Jumps] And don't come back!
RHINO. [Jumping] You come back into our jungle, and I'll
     trample you! [He illustrates.]
KING COBRA. [Jumps] And I'll **bite** you! [Illustrates]
ELEPHANT. And I'll sit on you! [Illustrates with a thud.]
LITTLE MONKEY NO. 1. [Climbing on top of ELEPHANT]
     Having a hunter in the jungle is worse than a **hundred** tigers.
LITTLE MONKEY NO. 2. You're right!
ELEPHANT. Wait a minute, everybody! Where is Jerome
     Tiger?
BIRD OF PARADISE. [Looking] And Big Monkey?
RHINO. Where are they?

[They are all searching about, when a great roar and
a tremendous monkey-screech come from offstage. JER-
OME runs on in full flight, pursued by **BIG MONKEY**
who carries the can of paint and the paint brush and the
folded umbrella which he is shaking like a stick.]

KING COBRA. Jerome Tiger!
RHINO. Where have you two been?
JEROME. [Fleeing in circles] Don't ask stupid questions, **save**
     me! Help! Help!
BIG MONKEY. [Waving the umbrella] Get back here, Jerome!
     I only want to help you!

JEROME. [Running right up to BIG MONKEY] That's what
    I said! **Help!** [He flees to the other animals, crouches and
    hides between their legs.]
BIRD OF PARADISE. What's wrong, Jerome?
ELEPHANT. [Nervous] I hope it's nothing upsetting!
BIG MONKEY. [To JEROME] Come on out here, you big
    sissy! [Waving the umbrella] I'm not going to hit you!
JEROME. Then what's the stick for?
KING COBRA. Wait a minute, everybody, **wait a minute!**
    [The commotion halts.] All right, Big Monkey, all right,
    Jerome Tiger, what's this all about? I thought everything
    was all settled.
BIG MONKEY. I just offered to paint Jerome calico again,
    that's all. Because when he was calico he was everybody's
    friend, and I wanted him to be **my** friend. See? [Opening
    the umbrella] I even brought him an umbrella so when the
    rainy season came he wouldn't have to worry about the
    paint washing off. But Jerome got all angry and started
    running, so I had to run after him to explain!
KING COBRA. Jerome, what do you say to that?
JEROME. I don't **want** to be a calico tiger. I don't want any
    of that sticky paint all over me. If I'm going to be liked,
    and you're all going to be my friends, I want you to like
    me, not something all painted up. I'm **me**. Don't you like
    me just as Jerome Tiger?
RHINO. I like you, Jerome.
BIRD OF PARADISE. And I like you.
LITTLE MONKEYS. [Together] And we like you!
ELEPHANT. Oooh, Jerome, I like you so much I think I'm
    going to cry!
BIG MONKEY. Yes, Jerome, I think you're right.
KING COBRA. I think we should like you because you're
    you.
BIRD OF PARADISE. You were very pretty when you were
    calico. Won't you maybe wear it on Sundays, just for me?
JEROME. [Flattered] Well, maybe. **If** I feel like it.

KING COBRA. Our problem is solved! We all like Jerome
    Tiger because he's **Jerome**, not because he's striped or
    calico . . .
JEROME. . . . But because I'm the friendliest tiger in the
    whole jungle!
KING COBRA. Three cheers for Jerome! Hip-Hip!
ALL. Hooray!
KING COBRA. Hip-Hip!
ALL. Hooray!
JEROME. [Thrilled] Gee!
KING COBRA. Hip-Hip!
ALL. **Hoo-ray!** [All cheer, run, jump and shake JEROME's
    hand.]

CURTAIN

www.ingramcontent.com/pod-product-compliance
Ingram Content Group UK Ltd.
Pitfield, Milton Keynes, MK11 3LW, UK
UKHW021910060726
6981IPUK00004B/59